To Diana

With many thanks and
much appreciation for all
your work!

Jim

Jan. 1990

Princess Navina Visits Malvolia

From the diary of

Count Nef

Drawings by Diana Schuppel Reid

LYTTON PUBLISHING COMPANY
S A N D P O I N T • I D A H O

Copyright ©1990 Lytton Publishing Company
ISBN 0-915728095

Direct inquiries to:
Lytton Publishing Company
335 Lavina Ave.
Sandpoint, Idaho 83864
208--263-3564

Publisher's note: *Many years ago, King Hobart Hollenstein, ruler of the Duchy of Pancratica, sent his heir apparent, the Princess Navina, on a world tour to study the governments of other lands. The king believed that the understanding of foreign customs to be gained from such a journey was the best possible preparation for a future monarch. In command of the touring party was the princess's beloved "Uncle Koko," known to the rest of the court as Baron Kolshic, the king's trusted Minister of Cotillion and Foreign Relations. Fortunately for posterity, a record of the journey was kept by Count Nef, a minor member of the entourage. This account of Malvolia is excerpted from his diary of the princess's travels.*

On the day before we sighted land, the baron informed the princess of the next disembarkation on our tour.

"Malvolia?" said the princess. "Why is it called that?"

"Because," replied the baron, "it is a land where the monarch wishes his subjects ill. It is apparently his policy to cause harm to his people."

"How horrible!" said the princess. "But why should I visit such a country? Do you wish me to learn how to make my dear Pancraticans miserable?" The princess seldom let pass an opportunity to tease the baron on political subjects.

"Of course not, Navi," he replied. "We are going to Malvolia so that you may learn what **not** to do as a ruler."

The Malvolian capital of Lamento, its commerce with the outside world being but slight, has no docks or port facilities. We therefore lay at anchor in the harbor for two days while the baron made the necessary arrangements on shore. On the third day following our landfall we set out with the princess for her audience with the magog.

We were apprehensive as we took our places in the long boat. From afar, Lamento looked attractive enough, nestled under brick-red cliffs that rose to the azure sky. But the baron had brought back disturbing intelligence of the place. The inhabitants, he had reported, were impoverished to an extreme, and also surly and hostile to visitors. Far from expecting a courteous welcome, we found ourselves fingering our scabbards and testing the freedom of our swords as the sailors rowed us across the bay.

At the landing, we saw the truth of the baron's reports, for the site was beset with miserable, rag-shrouded beggars, raucously clamoring for alms. As we disembarked and made our way through the throng, some members of our party gave out small gold pieces, hoping to win the affection of the rabble. Far from appeasing the supplicants, however, these acts of kindness only provoked louder imprecations—some of which reached even the ears of the princess herself!

With much relief we gained the security of the carriages and were conveyed thence to the castle — wondering all the while why the magog had permitted a reception so humiliating to the princess, and so unflattering to his kingdom. We were soon to learn the answer.

The audience with the seventeenth magog of Malvolia took place in the Hall of Mirrors. The magog did not lack regal presence, draped as he was in a black and white-striped zebra cape and standing tall over his subordinates. (It was not until later that we learned this effect was achieved by his underlings standing with their knees always doubled.)

As the introductions were made, we noticed that the baron identified our duchy as the "Empire of Pancratica," an appellation that puzzled us then, but the wisdom of which we were later to see.

After the formalities were completed, the princess began her interview by asking the magog about his kingly principles.

"My dear," replied the magog, "in Malvolia we rulers have one principle and one principle only, and that is to make everyone as unhappy as possible."

The audience with the seventeenth magog of Malvolia

"I have heard something to that effect," she replied, "but I don't really understand it."

"Sorrow, misfortune, distress," said the magog. "Call it what you will, that is the aim of the magog and of every submagog who serves me. We strive for the greatest misery for the greatest number."

"But why should you adopt such a, such a **frightful** doc—"

"Stop!" the magog interrupted. "You are guests in our land. You shall not be permitted to abuse our hospitality by questioning our sacred traditions."

The baron intervened. "We understand, Your Excellency. It is but our purpose to study your institutions, not"—he turned to the princess—"to comment upon them." Addressing the magog, he said, "Pray tell us what policies you follow to carry out your goal of making everyone unhappy."

The magog's anger dropped away. His eyes lit up and he rubbed his hands together. "Ah," he said with delight.

"Our policies of the modern era, that is, since my father, the sixteenth magog, differ radically from those of prior generations. The early magogs followed a simple policy. They undertook direct injury of the citizens. Burning was their favorite idea. They would periodically order the burning of crops, and barns, and places of habitation.

"These superficial measures did produce some momentary unhappiness, but they had two disadvantages. First, in responding to the adversity thus caused, the character of the citizens was strengthened. They would redouble their efforts and rebuild what had been destroyed. In so doing, they improved their own self-regard and thus laid the basis for their long-run happiness.

**"They would periodically order
the burning of crops, and barns, and places of habitation"**

"The second disadvantage of the policy of burning was its threat to the dynasty. As the citizens could see that the magog was directly responsible for the injury, these acts of destruction continually fed the spirit of revolt. Hence royal burnings could be engaged in but sparingly. Today, of course, we do no burning whatsoever," said the magog proudly.

"How then," asked the baron, "do you make your subjects unhappy—as we have seen they certainly are!"

The magog beamed at what he took to be a compliment. "Now we get to the heart of the matter." He paused for dramatic effect. "Negamos!"

"I beg your pardon?" said the baron.

"Negamos," repeated the magog. "We have adopted the policy of negamos. That is the foundation of misery in Malvolia."

"What, exactly, is a 'negamo'?" asked the baron.

"The name is taken from one of our rivers, Baron. Perhaps I should explain how it came about."

"Please do," said the baron, "for it sounds most interesting."

"It happened in the fall of the twenty-second year of

the rule of my father. It was a time of great ferment. My father had carried out some burnings that summer, in fact, quite a bit more than usual. He had destroyed two villages, as well as most of the maize crop. As a result, the citizens were particularly hostile. One Tuesday afternoon, my father went out in his carriage to survey his holdings in West Nomia. On returning, at the bridge that crosses the Negamo River, he encountered a band of peasants blocking the way.

"'Give us alms,' they cried. 'We have no food and our houses are burned down.'

"Naturally such words were music to my father's ears, and normally he would have made no move to alleviate the distress he had so carefully cultivated. But the peasants crowded 'round the carriage and began to shake it and beat upon it. Fearful for his own safety, my father threw some coins out the window to the rabble. The peasants quickly gathered them up, but still they maintained their position blocking the bridge.

"'Why won't you let me pass?' asked my father. 'I have given you the alms you sought.'

"One peasant stepped forward and addressed my

"Fearful for his own safety,
my father threw some coins out the window"

father. 'You have assisted us today, but what about next week? Next week you will be fat and warm in your castle and we shall be starving again.' He shook his fist at my father. 'You will forget us.' Thereupon the mob began to crowd against the carriage in a most menacing fashion. My father shouted, 'No, wait! I shall not forget you. On my oath as a magog, I pledge I shall return. One week hence, I will return to this very spot. If you are again in want and miserable, I shall again assist you.' Hearing these words, the crowd relented and allowed my father's carriage to escape across the bridge.

"At first, my father had no intention of honoring his promise to return the following week — and, of course, he was in no way bound to do so. In fact, our royal literature specifically counsels against such behavior. The **Sixth Book of Magogery,** for example, says 'As the alligator sweetly sings, so let the magog's oath be everlasting.'

"But although there was no moral basis to return to the banks of the Negamo, there was a practical one. The kingdom was in a precarious state. Hostile citizens were assaulting his royal officers, even in broad daylight. His spies were bringing in daily reports of conspiracies against the throne. While the state of popular discontent gratified my father's magogic principles, he realized that there were practical limits to idealism. A failure to keep his pledge, he saw, could easily become the spark to ignite a full-scale rebellion.

"On the following Tuesday, therefore, he went back to the Negamo and confronted the crowd—which was much larger than before. 'Are you still miserable and in want?' he asked. At once members of the crowd began moaning and cursing. 'We have no food,' cried one. 'There is no work in all the land,' shouted another. 'Our clothes are rags,' moaned a third. So again, my father distributed coins, and again promised to return the following Tuesday.

"This continued for many weeks, with my father returning to the Negamo and giving assistance to those who proclaimed their distress. As time passed, the crowds got larger and seemed more and more miserable. The people came in rags and without sandals. Some even cut their bodies to show their suffering.

"Other useful things began to happen. A delegation of farmers came to him to complain about the lack of laborers. Workers, having been given money by my father at the bridge, were not presenting themselves to till the fields and milk the cows. Those that did come were undisciplined and surly, practically daring their employers to discharge them: 'The magog will take care of us,' they jeered at the foremen.

"A delegation of women came from one of the villages to petition about the alms policy. 'Our husbands are becoming shiftless and lazy,' they complained. 'They know they need not work. Now they spend their time with wine, and wenches. Their self-respect is taken away and they grow angry at each other, and at us. And now our sons, seeing no need of mastering a trade, are taking after them.'

"Then my father saw that he had at last achieved what magogs had struggled for generations to achieve: a durable policy for promoting misery! Even though the revolutionary danger subsided the following spring, he did not cease his policy of returning to the bridge each Tuesday." The magog withdrew an orange handkerchief from his pocket and wiped his brow. "That," he said, "is how the negamo was discovered."

"I see," said the baron with measured politeness.

"Workers were undisciplined and surly,
practically daring their employers to discharge them"

"Then the negamo is a grant of money, is that so?"

"Not just any grant, my dear Baron," said the magog. The negamo is a grant **for being distressed**."

"And do you still go out in your carriage each Tuesday to give out this money?" asked the baron.

The magog laughed. "Goodness no. It would be impossible. We have nearly one million inhabitants in Malvolia, and half receive negamos. No, my father set up a system of booths in the villages where, every Tuesday, all supplicants who deem themselves sufficiently unhappy come to collect their grant. It all works quite smoothly. Generally all the negamos are distributed by midday, so as not to discourage anyone, by an undue wait, from applying."

At this point, the princess, who had been listening in stony silence to the magog's narration, entered the conversation. She had taken an immediate dislike to the magog and had resolved not to flatter him with questions. But now she saw a way to confute him without directly arousing his anger. "But surely," she said, "the people who come for these negamos might actually be quite content. They might simply be pretending to be unhappy in order to collect the money."

"My father set up a system of booths in the villages"

The magog was not at all displeased by her question. "Your Princess Navina," he said, winking to the baron, "has the instincts of a true statesman. She knows the tricks that the people will play. Yes, my dear," he said, turning back to her, "there was some tendency toward fraud at first. But my father was too clever. He first took jesters with him to the Negamo, to tell jokes and to do tricks, and he watched the reaction of the supplicants. And any who laughed, he had sent away without alms. Later, he employed a system of spies and agents to determine that the misfortune of the supplicants was real and not feigned. If their distress was found not to be genuine, they were excluded from the distribution of the negamo.

"This system of reporting, refined and expanded, is today the cornerstone of negamo policy. My people do not just play a role of being morose and sullen. They have learned to live it. As a result, even as I peek in windows and spy through hedges to catch people unawares, I can rarely find mirth or enthusiasm in any quarter."

"Any who laughed, he had sent away without alms"

The magog obviously expected a compliment, but the princess only pursed her lips and looked away.

To smooth over a tense moment, the baron said, "Your system seems most interesting, but tell us, how do you finance it? Surely paying all these negamos must cost a great deal of money."

"So far," said the magog, "the royal mint has been able to keep up. We have just added a ninth stamping machine, which is capable of producing sixty thousand mals an hour. If you have time on your visit here, you really ought to see this machinery."

"Mals?" said the princess. "What's a mal?" Her curiosity overcame her resolution to snub the man.

"The mal? That's our unit of currency. Page! Show the princess a mal."

The page came forward and handed the princess a coin. It was of dull grey metal and had a replica of a skull prominently displayed. The princess studied the inscription on the coin. Her brow furrowed. "What is it made of?" she asked.

"Lead," said the magog, "and five per cent antimony for hardness."

"Even as I peek in windows to catch people unawares,
I can rarely find mirth or enthusiasm in any quarter"

The princess frowned again. "But it says here, on the coin, 'perfectly pure gold.'"

"So what?"

"Well, I mean, why does it say it's gold if it's lead?"

"I suppose," replied the magog, "that it's just traditional. The earlier mals, before the days of my father, were made of gold and we have kept that inscription. Surely it doesn't matter. Money is just a medium of exchange. It's just superstition that money ought to be gold or silver or something valuable like that."

The princess said nothing, but it was clear that she was not satisfied.

"And besides," continued the magog, "we couldn't possibly make our mals out of gold. There wouldn't even begin to be enough. You see, we have to constantly increase our production of mals. It's the only way to keep up with the extreme inflation we have here."

"Inflation?" said the baron.

"Yes indeed, my dear Baron. Since the days of my father, the price of everything has risen enormously. No one seems to understand why. A loaf of bread, for example, used to cost two mals. Now it's over two hundred. This inflation makes it necessary to increase the negamo time and again, or it would cease to serve its purpose. Over the past fifty-five years, the negamo has been raised from 13 mals to 1,200—actually it is 1,225 this week. Obviously, to cover this increase we must increase our production of mals. Of course," the magog added as an afterthought, "we do get some income from the prosperity fines, but that's hardly significant."

"Did you say 'prosperity fines?'" asked the baron.

"We call them prosperity fines, but I prefer to think of them as dreaming fines," replied the magog. "You can't measure their contribution to unhappiness in terms of the mals taken from the populace."

"I'm afraid I don't understand," said the baron. "I haven't heard of a prosperity fine before."

"My goodness, your system of political economy must indeed be backward if you have not heard of a prosperity fine," said the magog. "For us, the idea originated with the third magog. In many ways, the discovery of this policy took the same path as the discovery of the negamo. It was a temporary expedient to combat rebellion, which was later retained for its long-term advantages.

A Malvolian mal

"It began as a strategy by the third magog to divert hostility from the dynasty. He went out and told angry workers and peasants that the real reason why they lacked wheat and maize was not due to the royal burnings. Instead, he told them, it was the wealthy who were responsible for their poverty. 'Their barns are bulging with corn,' he declaimed, 'and they burn wheat in their ottavars to spite the misery of the people. Is this just?' Of course the crowd thought not, and the magog made a pledge to them: 'Upon each of the rich shall I levy a fine, and each fine in due proportion to the prosperity of each. And the funds thus raised I shall distribute unto you.'

"It was another rare instance in the history of Malvolia when a magog actually kept his promise. The magog confiscated the property of the wealthy in proportion to their substance, and distributed some of it to the rest of the people. When the rebellion passed, he stopped the distribution, but he retained the system of proportional fines for its beneficial effect in vexing the wealthy.

"Later, in the fifteenth century, the great social philosopher, Nauseo the Elder, discovered more profound benefits of the prosperity fine. He pointed out that it discourages production, innovation, and saving. You see, under it, people are progressively penalized for making more income. That is, they are penalized for whatever creative work they do: raising corn, making watches, building dontiefs. Obviously, then, these productive labors are discouraged and as a result, society has less corn, fewer watches, and fewer dontiefs. In this way, the prosperity fine lays an excellent foundation for misery.

"But"—the magog was perspiring with the enthusiasm of his narration—"that isn't all. Nauseo pointed out that there was a hidden depressing effect of the prosperity fine, an effect on dreams and aspirations. You see, for everyone who actually succeeds in any risky, difficult venture, there are thousands who are only dreaming about such conquests. They are kept going by the slim hope that they, too, might make their dream come true. There are farmers hoping to develop a supermaize; inventors pursuing the possibility of a flying machine; writers scribbling away in their garrets, aspiring to write the great Malvolian novel. Their dreams and hopes give them a sense of purpose.

"The prosperity fine undermines these dreams. It

A dontief
(public transportation in Malvolia)

makes it impossible to dream of future wealth. The individual knows that even if he succeeds against the odds and at great sacrifice, the government will rob him of the fruits of his labors. As a result, creative and energetic people in Malvolia are particularly frustrated and morose. Really," said the magog, addressing the baron, "if you don't have a prosperity fine in your Empire of Pancratica, you surely should get one."

The magog again blotted his forehead with his orange handkerchief. He assumed his listeners were dumbfounded in admiration. "The manner in which we collect the prosperity fine," he continued, "adds a further nuance of frustration. We require that each person calculate his own fine, which might not be too difficult except for one thing." He paused, his eyes brimming with sneaky delight. "Except for the fact that the rules and regulations for computing the fines are immensely complex and illogical! This means that everyone has to work long and hard to try to figure out what their fine is, always haunted by the fear of doing it incorrectly and going to jail.

"So you see," he said, "we have at last contrived the perfect administration of unhappiness here in Malvolia. Our less energetic citizens are maintained in idleness and despair through the system of negamos. And they blame their misery not on the dynasty, but on the more productive citizens who, in turn, are harassed and frustrated by our prosperity tax. Discontent prevails at all levels, and yet our dynasty remains unchallenged."

"Are there no revolutionaries in Malvolia?" asked the baron.

"Not to any significant degree," replied the magog. "Of course, there are always a few hotheaded lads, but they have no following among the people."

The princess could contain herself no longer. Under her breath she made a sound.

"What was that, my dear?" asked the magog. He had failed to detect her growing hostility.

"Shocking!" said the princess in a louder voice. The baron gave her a warning glance, but she threw caution to the winds. "What you are doing to your people is simply shocking!" she declared.

The magog's eyes bulged as he grasped the meaning of her words. "In Malvolia, it is a capital offense to contradict our philosophy. Guards! Arrest Princess Navina!"

The baron stepped forward. "Stay a moment. Your Excellency would be most ill-advised to take action such as this. Such a deed could easily end in war with our empire."

"War?" said the magog. "What care I about war? All that would do is make my people more miserable. I would welcome a war with your Empire of Pancratica."

"But," said the baron, "surely you must realize that this war, if it should come about, would produce the destruction of your dynasty. When the empire I represent defeats you, we would certainly replace you with rulers who had the welfare of the Malvolian people at heart."

"Ah," said the magog. "That is a point worth considering." He paused. "But how would your empire fight such a war in any case? Your brigantine in the harbor, I am told, is unarmed."

The magog was correct on that point. The Duchy of Pancratica, being landlocked, has no navy at all. The vessel in which we sailed had been hired from a merchant firm in Genoa. The baron was indeed in a close pass. But he was equal to the challenge.

"Your Excellency, we are but the advance messenger of the Pancratic armada. In three days, they will overtake us and then you will see the Bay of Lamento white with sails of our warships."

The vividness of the baron's description caused the magog to hesitate. Pressing his advantage, the baron made a proposal. "But let us not talk of war, Your Excellency. We have come to study your institutions. Surely you have more points to explain?"

"Yes indeed!" The magog's anger seemed to have dropped away. "I particularly wanted the princess to learn about our treatment of minorities. I was going to explain the subject tomorrow."

"There. You see?" said the baron. "I am sure the princess is most eager to learn about such things—and she could hardly do so if she was, er, confined. Why don't we, therefore, postpone this other matter until the armada arrives, and continue with the visit as planned?"

"Very well," said the magog. "But I must warn the princess not to repeat her outburst. Here in Malvolia you can criticize our policies, but not our assumptions."

The princess nodded stiffly at him with a forced smile, and on this uncertain note, the audience with the magog was concluded.

As we went to the main gate of the castle, the princess whispered to the baron, "I hate that man! And he has such **dreadful** taste. Imagine, an orange handkerchief! Uncle Koko, let us go to the ship and sail at once."

"No, my dear," replied the baron. "We are being watched. If we make any attempt to flee, the magog will know my story of the armada is a bluff, and we shall all be arrested at once. No, we must go on with the visit quite naturally and wait for an opportune moment to slip away."

The princess bit her lip.

"And you, Navi, must behave with greater self-control. After all," he said, with a twinkle in his eye, "as it says in our royal code, 'The angry princess never charmed the singing alligator.'"

The princess giggled. "We don't have any royal code. Uncle Koko, you're so silly."

The castle gate is inconvenient

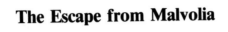

The Escape from Malvolia

he lodgings that the magog had arranged for us at the Olde Ache Royal Hostel were not entirely to our liking. The rooms were bare, damp and musty-smelling, and the tiny windows refused to open. Particularly irritating were the water faucets. When opened, no water came out. Naturally, after trying them, one left them open. Later, when one had forgotten, the water suddenly surged out with enormous force, splashing across the room and drenching whomever approached to shut the faucet. When turned on a few moments later, water would again refuse to flow.

In the room reserved for the princess, she found an enormous bed covered with a down mattress fully five feet thick. When she first saw it, she exclaimed with delight at its softness, praising it over the sturdy bunks of the ship.

She was to regret her words, however. When she tried to sleep on it, she sank too deeply down, so that the mattress engulfed her and made her perspire. Furthermore, her arms and legs were pinned in the deep cleft of the mattress, so that she could not stir or turn in any direction. Many times during the night she crawled out of the bed to pace the floor, only to be driven back to the bed by the sound of mice scurrying across the floor.

After passing such a night in this abominable hostel, it was understandable that the princess was not in the best of humor when we returned to the castle the next day.

The magog again received us in the Hall of Mirrors, seated comfortably on his gilded sillonte. "And how did you pass the night, my dear?" he asked the princess. He seemed to have forgotten his anger of the day before.

The princess, showing her good breeding, only said, "Very well, thank you."

The magog seemed disappointed. "Really? Are you sure there wasn't some discomfort?"

"Well, if you really want to know," said the princess hotly, "I spent the most disagreeable night of my life in that horrid bed!"

The mattress engulfed her and made her perspire

"Just as I expected," said the magog, slapping his thigh with delight.

"You mean you knew I would be uncomfortable?"

"But of course!"

"Why did you permit such a thing, then?"

"My dear, this is Malvolia. It is my duty to make everyone, even visitors unhappy."

The princess stamped her foot. "Well, why didn't you just. . . just burn the hostel down if you wanted to make me unhappy?"

The magog was undisturbed by her petulant tone. "Ah, my dear, a fire would have been so old-fashioned, and also counterproductive. Suppose that you had escaped with your life. Then you would have had a delightful tale of adventure to recount to your children and grandchildren, making them, and you, happy in the telling of it. But what tale is there to tell about passing an uncomfortable night in a bed too soft?"

"But suppose I died in the fire?" asked the princess.

"Then you would be dead, not unhappy. Dead people are not unhappy. For this reason, in Malvolia we avoid killing anybody, except revolutionaries, and visitors who

"Why didn't you just burn the hostel down
if you wanted to make me unhappy?"

contradict our philosophies"—he looked pointedly at the baron—"without armadas to back them up."

"Be that as it may," said the baron, quickly changing the subject. "We understand you wished to explain your minorities policy today. We are most anxious to learn of your treatment of this problem."

"Yes, indeed," replied the magog, apparently forgetting his threat. It seemed that whenever he turned to discuss policy subjects, the magog became a changed man, fully engrossed in the delights of administrative theory.

"Our minorities policy began with the fourteenth magog. He had learned from travellers about the problems with minorities that existed in the Austral-Hungovian Empire." He turned to the baron. "You have heard of that kingdom?"

"It is a small realm lying to the southwest of our empire," said the baron, always careful to sustain the image of Pancratica's greatness.

"The fourteenth magog learned that minorities were a great source of misery and resentment in that kingdom, and so he naturally wondered if it wouldn't be possible to bring this problem to Malvolia."

"Naturally," echoed the princess, but the magog missed her sarcasm.

"Unfortunately, Malvolia does not have any native minorities. Everyone here speaks the same language and shares the same culture and religion, and so forth. Therefore, in order to have a minority problem, the magog saw he would have to create a minority artificially.

"He began with the ems, that is, everyone whose last name begins with the letter **m**. All such people were made the object of special discriminatory legislation. They were not permitted to attend the university; they could not ride in the public dontiefs; they were forbidden to take part in the professional dugeball contests; and they had to pay a special yearly fine of, if I recall rightly, fifty mals.

"Of course, the ems were injured by these measures, and to this degree one could say the policy succeeded. But, as so often happened with the ancient magogian policies, there were side effects that nullified the original intent.

"First, in order to overcome the disadvantage laid upon them, the ems became particularly industrious. They worked longer hours in the shops and fields, and trained their children to be frugal and hardworking. Thus, they

"Others helped found and sustain the Em University"

developed healthy attitudes that laid the foundation for their future success.

"Second, many non-ems began to sympathize with the ems and acted to counteract the injustice against them. Some non-ems went out of their way to employ ems, others helped found and sustain the Em University, and many took up a campaign against the dynasty to repeal the laws discriminating against ems. Thus, the em policy became a source of hostility toward our rule.

"Matters continued in this unsatisfactory state until my father, the sixteenth magog, took up the matter. He had discovered, with his negamo, the great principal of social decay, that misery is fostered by a regularized system of granting unmerited benefits. He applied this insight to the minority issue, and realized that he needed to reverse the existing policy. He abolished all discriminatory legislation and replaced it with positive measures designed to confer an advantage on ems. He instituted a fine of seventy mals against anyone who failed to give employment to an em. He reserved two hundred places at the University of Malvolia for em students. And he began a special, extra negamo, called the "negamem," of six mals, given only to ems.

"As a result, hostility has increased marvelously. The non-ems increasingly resent the special treatment of ems. Gone are sentiments of sympathy and brotherhood. The ems, for their part, now look to the dynasty, instead of their own efforts, for their social improvement, and expend their energies constantly agitating for an increase in the negamem."

"But surely," asked the baron, "the ems are aware of their special treatment, are they not? They must see through this effort to subvert them."

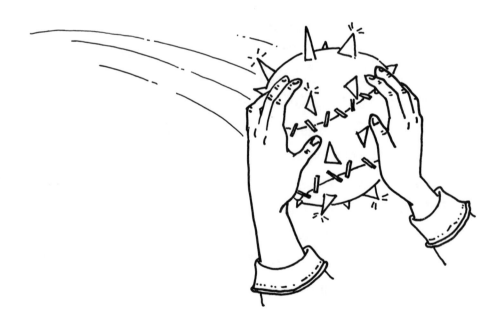

A Malvolian dugeball
(It hurts if you don't catch it right)

"Yes and no, Baron. They are aware of the special legislation, but they view it as a just corrective for their particular problems. One must never underestimate a social group's capacity to convince itself that it suffers a special disadvantage requiring governmental redress."

"Why don't they just change their names to begin with some letter instead of **m**?" asked the princess.

"That's administratively impossible," replied the magog. "We keep extensive records in Malvolia. Each person's name is entered in scores of governmental files and lists, too many to track down and alter.

"This is not to say we have rested on our laurels concerning the creation of minorities," continued the magog. "Some years ago, the ens began agitating to be included under em legislation, arguing that they resembled ems and faced similar problems. So we extended the policy to them. Next January, we will extend the policy to ohs and pees. It is our long-run objective to turn all our citizens into specially treated minorities, so that everyone will resent everyone else." He turned to the baron. "If you stay in Malvolia long enough, Baron, we shall even get to you with the letter **k**."

Records in Malvolia are very extensive—and hard to retrieve

The baron just smiled at the jest, but he also caught the barb that lay behind it. "Most interesting indeed, Your Excellency." He consulted his gold pocket watch. "My goodness," he exclaimed, "I'm afraid it's time to conclude our audience. The princess is much fatigued and. . . ."

The magog appeared to accept the point. "But you will return tomorrow to see our mint?" he asked.

"Oh yes, indeed," replied the baron. "We wouldn't want to miss seeing your new stamping machine."

Thus we took our leave of the magog once again. The royal party repaired to the hostel to review a situation that was growing more desperate by the minute. There was no Pancratic armada, of course, and the magog was becoming ever more skeptical of the baron's bluff. It seemed only a matter of time before we were all arrested and perhaps even executed by the villain who ruled this forsaken land.

Shortly after sunset, our fortunes took a turn for the better. There entered the hostel a youth, dressed in peasant garb, who demanded to see the princess. He had, he said, a message concerning her safety which he would deliver only to her. His request was unusual, but so were the circumstances in which we found ourselves. After some hesitation, the baron and I took the lad up to the princess's chamber.

He introduced himself to her. "My name is Lare Bil, Your Highness. I am a junior tutor at the university and have donned these rustic garments as a disguise. I come to warn you that you are in the greatest danger. The magog intends to arrest you and your entire company this very night!"

"Oh dear," said the princess. "What shall we do?"

Before the boy could speak, the baron interposed. "How do you know this, and why have you taken the trouble to warn us?"

"I am the leader of the Committee for Deconstructing Malvolian Dysfunctions," he replied. "We are enemies of the magog and are sworn to overthrow him. We learned of his intentions against you from one of our spies in the magog's castle.

"You must flee to your ship at once," he continued. "The magog has posted guards in front of the hostel, but you may escape through the coal cellar. I can lead you through the back alleys so that you may reach your ship before he learns of your escape. But you must hurry!"

**"I am the leader of the
Committee for Deconstructing Malvolian Dysfunctions"**

There seemed to be no alternative but to trust him. Orders were given to prepare for our departure from the hostel.

While the trunks were being packed, the princess engaged the young man in conversation. Even though dressed as a peasant, he was a handsome youth with a winsome smile and flowing golden hair.

"It is very good of you, and brave of you, to help us in this way. You seek to overthrow the magog, do you?"

"Yes, Your Highness. We shall not rest until the dynasty is destroyed."

"I do admire you for it," she replied. "No undertaking could be more noble than to destroy that horrid man! Tell me, Lare, what policies do you intend to follow after you have overthrown the magog?"

His face lit up with enthusiasm. "We have discussed this question night after night at our meetings at the university. Our first and most important measure, when we come to power, will be to increase the negamo! As it is today, the people of Malvolia are practically starving on the negamo of 1,225. Why, with inflation being what it is, 1,225 mals is barely enough to keep body and soul together."

"I see," said the princess. "But tell me, Lare, how do you intend to pay the cost of this increased negamo?"

"We have thought of that, too," he replied. "We shall enact a tax on the wealthy, a tax that increases in proportion to each person's income."

"But doesn't the magog already tax the wealthy?"

"Oh no, no, no. Not at all! He has a system of **fines**. We are talking about a **tax**."

"What's the difference?" asked the princess.

"Well, it's. . . it's obvious. A fine, I mean, a fine is unfair, a tax is fair."

At that moment, the conversation had to be interrupted by our departure. Lare led the princess and the rest of our company to the basement and out through the coal cellar. Of course, wriggling out the narrow chute begrimed our clothes with carbon, but this was a small price to pay for our deliverance. Ever so quietly, we followed our guide through a series of twisting alleys and paths. Soon we reached the beach where the long boat, unguarded, was lying drawn up on the sand.

Before she climbed aboard, the princess took Lare's hand and squeezed it tightly. "May God go with you," she

**Lare led the princess and the rest of our company
out through the coal cellar**

said, looking into his eyes. Then she stood on her tiptoes
and surprised the lad with a kiss on the cheek.

As soon as we reached the brigantine, the anchor
cables were cut and we glided out of the harbor to the open
sea. The princess remained on the taffrail, waving, until all
sight of land was gone.

Before retiring, we all toasted our deliverance from the
accursed land of Malvolia with a double measure of
carbingac.

The next morning, the baron and I were taking the sea air at the windward rail when the princess came on deck and joined us. She stood quietly for some time looking out over the heaving swell.

"Uncle Koko," she said suddenly, "what's the difference between a fine and a tax?"

"Well, er, I suppose one could say that a fine is unfair while a tax is fair."

"I know **that**," said the princess. "But why?"

The baron thought for a moment. "It's a question of motive, really. A fine is a type of punishment. The ruler who wishes to harm his subjects, like the magog of Malvolia, uses fines. The ruler who seeks to improve his kingdom uses taxes. For example, your father collects a ten dina tax from all who enter the royal capital city of Plotz. He collects this money not as a punishment—for he loves his subjects—but in order to maintain the royal stables. It's all a question of intentions."

"I think I see," said the princess slowly.

We stood in silence for a time, watching the gulls skim the waves. Then the princess addressed me. "Count, how can I send a letter to Lare?"

"Do you know his address, Princess?" I replied.

"Yes, he gave it to me last night, and I have put it on this letter here." She showed us a letter already sealed and addressed. "What I fear," she continued, "is that it won't be delivered. In that horrible Malvolia, they will reason that since it will give Lare pleasure, it must be denied him."

"A very good point, Princess," said I. "Let me think on the problem." In a flash, I saw the solution. "May I have the envelope, please."

She handed it over and, laying it upon the binnacle, I wrote an additional message upon it, alongside the address: "Warning! Contains tragic news. Do not open if discouraged or depressed." When the princess saw it, she astonished me with a hug, and said—these were her exact words—"Count, you are a prodigy!"